Goodnight
World

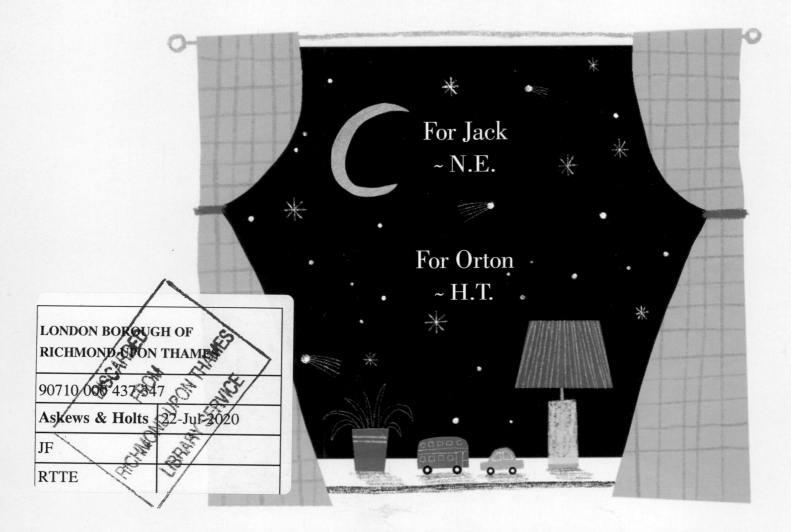

For Jack
~ N.E.

For Orton
~ H.T.

The pronunciations included in this book are supplied as a general
guide only, as some languages featured vary in the way they
are spoken across the world.

CATERPILLAR BOOKS

An imprint of the Little Tiger Group

www.littletiger.co.uk

1 Coda Studios, 189 Munster Road, London SW6 6AW

First published in Great Britain 2019

This edition published in 2020

Text by Nicola Edwards

Text copyright © Caterpillar Books Ltd 2019

Illustrations copyright © Hannah Tolson 2019

A CIP Catalogue record for this book is available from the British Library

All rights reserved • Printed in China

ISBN: 978-1-83891-036-5

CPB/1400/1410/0420

2 4 6 8 10 9 7 5 3 1

Goodnight World

Nicola Edwards

Illustrated by hannah tolson

LITTLE TIGER

LONDON

When the day's at an end, up to bed we will go,
The sky becomes dusky and so the night grows.

When the bright golden sun sheds the last of its light,
We turn to each other and we say, "Goodnight!"

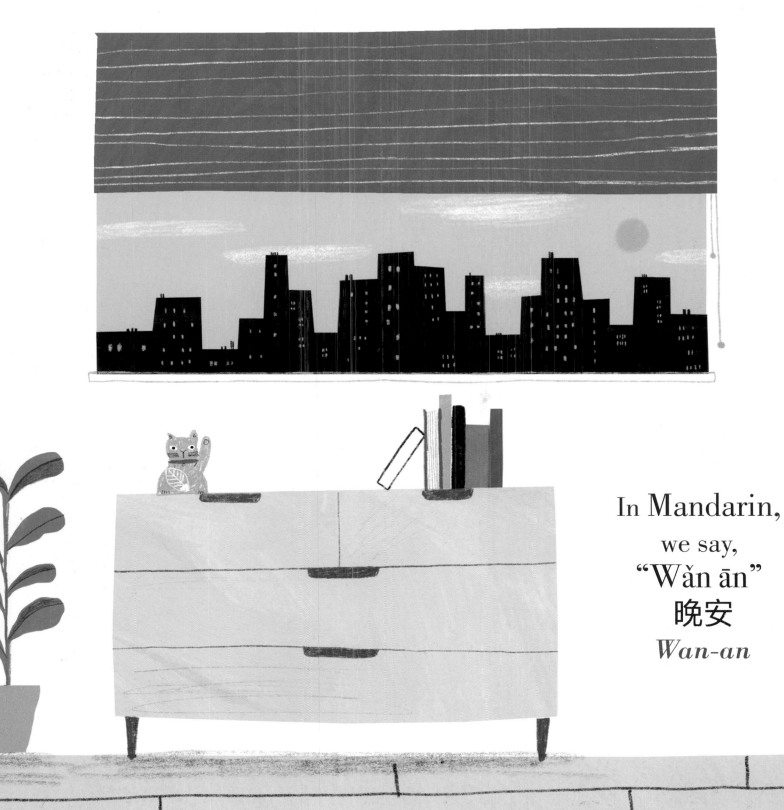

In Mandarin,
we say,
"Wǎn ān"
晚安
Wan-an

In the warmth of the bath we build towers of foam,

Rubber ducks bob along as we sail our boats home.

Then we're wrapped in a towel all ready for bed,
We get our "Goodnight!" and a kiss on the head.

In Russian,
we say,
"Spokoynoy nochi"
Спокойной ночи
Spok-oy-noy no-chi

In front of the mirror

we jostle for space,

We splish and we splash

and we make it a race.

We scrub up, then file out

and switch off the light,

We're ready for bed

and we all say, "Goodnight!"

In Italian, we say,
"Buona notte"
Bwon-na no-tay

All teddies get tired and the trains won't run late,

So the toys' next adventures will just have to wait.

We tidy our things up, make everything right

For more fun tomorrow. Until then, "Goodnight!"

In Finnish, we say,
"Hyvää yötä"
Hoo-vah ooh-er-tah

When we're far from our loved ones and it's time for bed,

A phone call replaces a kiss on the head.

That voice says "Goodnight!" and we don't feel so far,

Our "Goodnight!" finds you too, wherever you are.

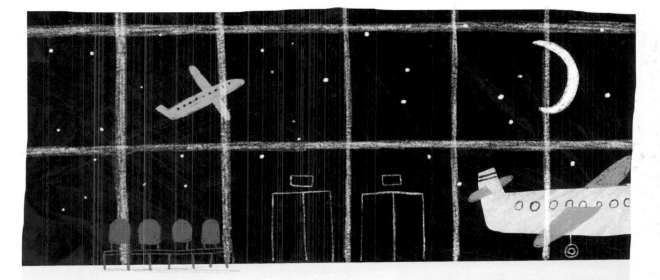

In Swahili, we say, "Usiku mwema"

Ooh-see-koo mweh-ma

When we're all here together,
we whisper and giggle,
And nobody minds
being squashed in the middle,

But soon it is time and we turn out the light,
In a chorus of one voice, we all say, "Goodnight!"

In Spanish, we say,
"Buenas noches"
Bwen-oss no-chez

Tonight there's a tale

from a faraway place,

With pirates, a princess,

a journey to space...

And slowly but surely

our eyes start to close,

We get our "Goodnight!"

and a kiss on the nose.

In Arabic, we say,
"Tisbah ala khair"
تصبح على خير
Tuss-bah el-la kher

When we've spent all our time just running about
And the day's wild adventures have worn us right out,

We're carried to bed, we're already asleep,

We get a "Goodnight!" but we don't hear a peep.

In Hindi, we say, "Shubh raatri"
शुभ रात्रि *Shub raa-tree*

We doze under canvas, by the light of the Moon,
Trees rustle above us, we'll be fast asleep soon.

Under blankets of stars, we are snuggled up tight,
In the peace of our tent we all whisper, "Goodnight!"

In German, we say,
"Gute nacht"
Goo-teh naakt

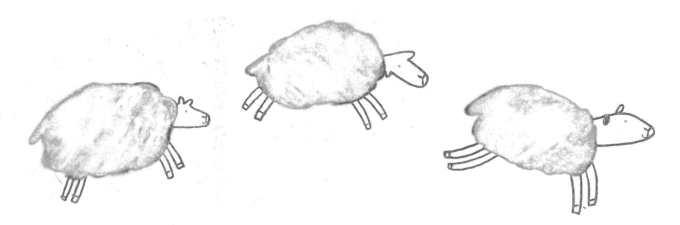

When those precious sweet dreams

just don't come right away,

Like the Sandman got lost

or his plan went astray,

If we can be patient

and count up those sheep,

Before long, "Goodnight!"

will be followed by sleep.

In French, we say,
"Bonne nuit"
Bon nwee

Bedtime is something that everyone shares,

From children to chicks, and from bunnies to bears.

We all get tucked in, from the big to the small,

And say our goodnights, one by one, each to all.

In Korean,
we say,
"Jal jayo"
잘 자요
Chai jai-yo

When the bright sun has set, up to bed we all go,

We cuddle up close when the moon is aglow.

We all have our dreams and we all say,

"Goodnight!"

In Spanish, we say,
"Buenas noches"

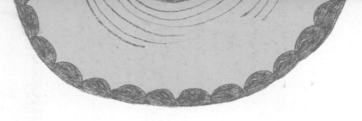

In Russian, we say,
"Spokoynoy nochi"

In Mandarin,
we say, "Wǎn ān"

In Korean,
we say,
"Jal jayo"

In French, we say,
"Bonne nuit"

In Italian, we say,
"Buona notte"

In Swahili, we say,
"Usiku mwema"

In Finnish, we say,
"Hyvää yötä"

"Goodnight!"

In Hindi, we say,
"Shubh raatri"

In German, we say,
"Gute nacht"